THE OFFICIAL
SUNDERLAND AFC
ANNUAL 2025

Written by Rob Mason & Barbara Mason
Designed by Mathew Whittles

With thanks to Kieran Regan, Kate Smith, Barry Jackson, Andrew Smithson, Ruby Smithson-Healy & Mike Gibson

A Grange Publication

© 2024. Published by Grange Communications Ltd., Edinburgh, under licence from Sunderland A.F.C. Printed in the EU.

Every effort has been made to ensure the accuracy of information within this publication but the publishers cannot be held responsible for any errors or omissions. Views expressed are those of the author and do not necessarily represent those of the publishers or the football club. All rights reserved.

Photographs © Alamy Live News, Ian Horrocks, Kasey Taylor, Ross Johnston RJX Media, Barbara Mason & Sunderland A.F.C.

ISBN 978-1-915879-93-6

JOBE

CONTENTS

SEASON REVIEW

Heavily deflected goals In the first two Championship fixtures led to 2-1 defeats and a poor start, but there was optimism that the play-offs could be reached for the second successive season. However, just as those key goals in the opening home and away games against Ipswich Town and Preston North End went against Sunderland, the 2023-24 season was to be a year where by and large the breaks went against the side. Hurt by a lot of long-term injuries and the lack of a goalscoring centre-forward, the players did well to stay in contention for a play-off place so far into the season. The hope and ambition for 2024-25 is to get Sunderland back into the Premier League.

AUGUST

PLAYED	WON	DRAWN	LOST
5	1	2	2

POSITION AT END OF MONTH: 18TH

Includes Carabao Cup game with Crewe Alexandra, lost on penalties after a 1-1 draw

KEY MOMENTS:
Chris Rigg became Sunderland's youngest ever scorer when netting against Crewe Alexandra. Rigg was only 16 years and 51 days. Rigg also wrote his name into national record books as he became the youngest scorer in the League (Carabao) Cup's history. In the next home game new signing Jobe scored both goals as Rotherham United were beaten in Sunderland's first win of the campaign.

SEPTEMBER

PLAYED	WON	DRAWN	LOST
5	4	0	1

POSITION AT END OF MONTH: 4TH

KEY MOMENTS:
Chris Rigg became Sunderland's youngest ever league scorer when completing a 5-0 rout of Southampton with a header to cap a superb 5-0 win in which Pierre Ekwah scored two long distance goals. Slaughtering the Saints was the highlight of a month where every game but one was won with the lone defeat at home to Cardiff City coming from a 1-0 loss to a late set-piece after Sunderland had dominated.

OCTOBER

PLAYED	WON	DRAWN	LOST
5	2	0	3

POSITION AT END OF MONTH: 7TH

KEY MOMENTS:
Dan Neil was very harshly sent off just before half-time in a home derby with Middlesbrough. After the interval score was level with Sunderland the better team, Boro took full advantage, going on to win 4-0 and set Sunderland off on a disappointing run. Fourth at the time, the team would never reach such a high position again all season.

NOVEMBER

PLAYED	WON	DRAWN	LOST
4	1	1	2

POSITION AT END OF MONTH: 11TH

KEY MOMENTS:
Jobe scored against his former club Birmingham City in a 3-1 win that lifted the Lads briefly back into the play-off positions, but there were back-to-back defeats at Swansea City and at home to Huddersfield Town, where the visitors performed a smash and grab raid to win 2-1 after Sunderland turned their 76% possession into 27 shots and 10 corners.

JANUARY

PLAYED	WON	DRAWN	LOST
5	2	0	3

Includes FA Cup tie with Newcastle United

POSITION AT END OF MONTH: 7TH

KEY MOMENTS:
A home FA Cup defeat by Newcastle United was a first defeat in ten meetings with the local rivals, but the match overshadowed much of the start of the year which had started brightly with a New Year's Day win over Preston North End. The month ended well with a home victory over Stoke City after narrow back to back league losses to Ipswich Town and Hull City.

FEBRUARY

PLAYED	WON	DRAWN	LOST
5	1	1	3

POSITION AT END OF MONTH: 10TH

KEY MOMENTS:
Following up a draw at Middlesbrough with a good home win over Plymouth Argyle, Sunderland were sixth but it was to be the last time in the season the team would occupy a play-off berth. The month ended with a trio of defeats and a change of head coach between the second and third of those as Michael Beale was dismissed and replaced by Mike Dodds who was installed as Interim head coach to the end of the season.

DECEMBER

PLAYED	WON	DRAWN	LOST
7	3	2	2

POSITION AT END OF MONTH: 7TH

KEY MOMENTS:
Head coach Tony Mowbray was sacked a couple of days after the opening game of the month at Millwall where a 1-1 draw left the side in ninth place, three points outside the play-off places. After Mike Dodds oversaw two excellent wins from three games in charge, former Queens Park Rangers and Rangers manager Michael Beale was appointed as the team's new head coach.

APRIL

PLAYED	WON	DRAWN	LOST
6	1	2	4

POSITION AT END OF MONTH: 15TH

KEY MOMENTS:
Twice as many goals were scored in the first game of the month than in the other five combined. Blackburn Rovers stunned the Stadium of Light with a 5-1 win but after that Sunderland tightened up, keeping three successive clean sheets with goalless draws against Bristol City and Leeds United followed by a 1-0 win at West Bromwich Albion. Pierre Ekwah's strike from a corner at WBA proved to be Sunderland's last goal of the season as the month ended with single goal defeats at the hands of Millwall and Watford.

MARCH

PLAYED	WON	DRAWN	LOST
5	1	1	3

POSITION AT END OF MONTH: 12TH

KEY MOMENTS:
Sunderland fielded the youngest starting XI in the club's history at Southampton, with the average age just 21 years and three days. They showed character and ability to come back from 2-0 down to draw level with Romaine Mundle's first for the club and a truly special shot from Jobe before Saint sub Joe Rothwell's late brace took the game away. Jobe was then outstanding at Cardiff City. Playing up front, he scored one and earned a penalty – tucked away by Adil Aouchiche – as a fine 2-0 win was recorded.

MAY

PLAYED	WON	DRAWN	LOST
1	0	0	1

POSITION AT END OF MONTH: 16TH

KEY MOMENTS:
A final day defeat to Sheffield Wednesday was enough to keep the Owls up but saw Sunderland slip to their lowest position since the opening month of the campaign. Sunderland wore white shorts in this game and changed their run out music to the theme from a very old TV series called Z-Cars which was the club's entrance music for several years at their old ground of Roker Park. This was in tribute to the club's Player of the Century Charlie Hurley who had recently passed away.

SEASON AWARDS

MEN'S PLAYER
OF THE SEASON:

JACK CLARKE

MEN'S PLAYERS' PLAYER
OF THE SEASON:

JACK CLARKE

WOMEN'S PLAYER
OF THE SEASON:

EMILY SCARR

WOMEN'S PLAYERS' PLAYER
OF THE SEASON:

CLAUDIA MOAN

The Beacon of Light, next to the Stadium of Light, staged a glamorous awards evening to honour the stars of the season in 2024. The evening featured Sunderland fan and rising pop star **Tom A. Smith**, who passionately performed a short set.

With all of the first team players from both the men's and women's squads in attendance along with club directors, the awards night was a very special high-class event.

Jack Clarke and **Emily Scarr** won the awards for the men's and women's Players of the Season with both making it a double. Clarke also won his teammates' vote as Players' Player of the Year while Scarr made it back-to-back Player of the Season awards. Goalkeeper **Claudia Moan** received the Players' Player of the Year for the women's side.

Jobe, Dan Neil, Dan Ballard, Trai Hume and Luke O'Nien were shortlisted for the Player of the Season accolade while Anthony Patterson joined Ballard and Hume in also being nominated for the Players' Player award. In the women's section Jenna Dear, Mary McAteer, Claudia Moan, Amy Goddard and Katie Kitching were all shortlisted for the Player of the Season honour while Scarr and Kitching joined Moan on the three-woman shortlist for the Players' Player award.

MEN'S YOUNG PLAYER
OF THE SEASON:

DAN NEIL

WOMEN'S YOUNG
PLAYER OF THE SEASON:

MARY McATEER

Dan Neil pipped Jobe, Trai Hume and Chris Rigg to the Young Player of the Season award for the men's team while in the women's awards **Mary McAteer** edged out Katy Watson, Jessica Brown and Grace Ede whose fine seasons also saw them nominated for the award.

Several other people also carried away special awards from the End of Season Awards Evening. **Pierre Ekwah** was a popular winner of the Community Player of the Season, **Chris Rigg** walked off with the Professional Development Player of the Season award and **Harry Wood** from the Under 11 team was named the Junior Player of the season.

A vote at the awards dinner saw **Niall Huggins'** brilliant slaloming run and finish into the top corner against Watford at the Stadium of Light named as the Goal of the Season. Other nominations for this were Jack Clarke v Sheffield Wednesday, Jobe v Southampton, Pierre Ekwah, also v Southampton, Mary McAteer, another against Southampton, Jenna Dear v Lewes and Katie Kitching goals against Durham and Reading.

The final award of the night brought a standing ovation for academy goalkeeping coach and former Sunderland goalkeeper **Mark Prudhoe**. 'Prud' won the award for Lifetime Achievement. A local lad from Washington, Mark first joined Sunderland in 1980 as a 17-year old. He made seven first team appearances before moving on to extend his career, being on the books of 18 different clubs, including loans. After moving into coaching he again worked for numerous clubs before coming full circle to Sunderland in 2011. Since then he has brought over 20 goalkeepers into the professional game, including Anthony Patterson and England's Jordan Pickford.

COMMUNITY PLAYER
OF THE SEASON:

PIERRE EKWAH

GOAL OF THE SEASON:

NIALL HUGGINS

PROFESSIONAL
DEVELOPMENT PLAYER
OF THE SEASON:

CHRIS RIGG

LIFETIME ACHIEVEMENT
AWARD:

MARK PRUDHOE

JUNIOR PLAYER
OF THE SEASON:

HARRY WOOD

STAT ATTACK

16 YEARS 51 DAYS

The age of Chris Rigg when he scored against Crewe Alexandra in the League (Carabao) Cup, making Chris the youngest scorer in Sunderland's history.

25

25 days after his first goal in a cup tie, Rigg scored against Southampton to become the club's youngest ever league goal-scorer. By the end of the season Rigg's 25 league appearances was also a record for a 16-year old.

1994-95

The last season when Sunderland played at Championship level without the season ending in promotion, play off defeat or relegation, until 2023-24. Since then, until last season, the Lads had been promoted four times, lost in the play-offs three times and been relegated once.

DARIUSZ KUBICKI

1914-15

For the first time since 1914-15 Sunderland won three successive away games with three goals scored in each of them. These were 3-1 wins at QPR and Blackburn Rovers followed by a 3-0 victory at Sheffield Wednesday.

55

The 4-2 defeat at Premier League bound Southampton in March was the first time in 55 away games that more than two goals had been scored against Sunderland. The Saints had suffered their heaviest defeat of the season when beaten 5-0 at the Stadium of Light earlier in the season.

59

To the start of the 2024-25 campaign it had been 59 away trips since Sunderland had been beaten by more than two goals in an away match.

90

Of the 90 away games Luke O'Nien has started in defence away from home (up to the start of the 2024-25 season) Sunderland have conceded more than two goals on only two occasions.

RIGG

O'NIEN

265

With 265 appearances up to the start of this season, Luke O'Nien has now played more games for Sunderland than anyone else so far this century.

132

O'Nien's first appearance at the Stadium of Light this season made him the player to have played most games for Sunderland at the stadium since it opened in 1997. John O'Shea and Lee Cattermole each made 131 but also added other games at the stadium for other clubs.

14

Sunderland scored the first goal in 14 Championship games in 2023-24. They won 12 of these games.

4

Sunderland won four and drew three of the 27 games where their opponents scored first in 2023-24.

30

Goals were conceded at home for the second consecutive season. This was the first time 30 goals have been conceded at home in back-to-back seasons outside of the top flight. Only once previously – in 1989-90 – had as many goals been scored against Sunderland on Wearside in 32 seasons spent in the second tier.

56

When he was only well enough to come on as a sub against Millwall in April, Trai Hume ended his run of 56 consecutive league appearances. This was the best run by an outfield player since another right back, Poland international Dariusz Kubicki, ended a 112 match run in 1996.

107

When goalkeeper Anthony Patterson was left on the bench for the final game of the 2023-24 season it ended a sequence of 107 league starts. This was the third best run in the entire history of the club who first played in the league in 1890. Only Dariusz Kubicki (112 games between 1994-96) and Charlie Thomson (134 between January 1934 and March 1937) have been longer runs of consecutive league appearances.

7

During 2024 Patterson became only the seventh player in the club's history to achieve a century of consecutive league appearances. He joined Dariusz Kubicki, Barry Siddall, George Mulhall, Charlie Thomson, Bert Davis and Sandy McAllister.

7

Seven players made 40 or more Championship appearances in 2023-24. This equalled the highest number ever for a 46 game season, set in the 2004-05 Championship winning season. Six of those seven players totalled over 40 starting appearances, a number which has never been matched.

2

Only two loan players appeared in 2023-24, the lowest since 2012-13 when Danny Rose was on loan from Tottenham Hotspur. Mason Burstow and Callum Styles from Chelsea and Barnsley were the loanees last season.

10

There were ten penalties in Sunderland's games in 2023-24, six for and four against. Sunderland scored all of their spot kicks with Anthony Patterson saving one of the penalties he faced.

15

Players made their first team debut during 2023-24.

CATTERMOLE

15

Jack Clarke was top scorer with 15 goals. Following Amad's 14 the season before this made it the second consecutive season that the top scorer had been a winger. 12 of Clarke's 15 goals were scored away from home.

1 & 90

Sunderland scored in the first and last minutes of a game for only the second time in the club's history. Jack Clarke and Chris Rigg opened and closed the scoring in a 5-0 win over Southampton. This was the first time Sunderland had ever scored in the opening and final minutes of a home game. The only time it had ever happened before was when Marco Gabbiadini scored the first two goals of his Sunderland career at Fulham in 1987.

21 YEARS 3 DAYS

The average age of the starting line-up at Southampton. This was the youngest team ever selected for a competitive game in the club's history.

O'SHEA

SUMMER SIGNINGS

WILSON ISIDOR

Position: Forward

Date of Birth: 27 August 2000

Age at the Start of the Season: 23

Birthplace: Rennes, France

Other Clubs: Rennes, Monaco, Laval (L), Bastia-Borgo (L), Lokomotiv Moscow, Zenit Saint Petersburg

International: France Under 20

2023-24 Appearances: 1+3 for Lokomotiv Moscow and 4+10 for Zenit Saint Petersburg

2023-24 Goals: 1 for Lokomotiv Moscow and 2 for Zenit Saint Petersburg

ALAN BROWNE

Position: Midfielder

Date of Birth: 15 April 1995

Age at the Start of the Season: 29

Birthplace: Cork

Other Clubs: Preston North End

International: Republic of Ireland

2023-24 Appearances: 43 for Preston plus 5 for the Republic of Ireland

2023-24 Goals: 4 for Preston

SIMON MOORE

Position: Goalkeeper

Date of Birth: 19 May 1990

Age at the Start of the Season: 34

Birthplace: Sandown

Other Clubs: Brading Town, Southampton, Farnborough, Brentford, Basingstoke Town (L), Cardiff City, Bristol City (L), Sheffield United, Coventry City

International: Isle of Wight

2023-24 Appearances: 0

2023-24 Goals: 0

IAN POVEDA

Position: Attacking midfielder or winger

Date of Birth: 9 February 2000

Age at the Start of the Season: 24

Birthplace: London

Other Clubs: Chelsea, Arsenal, Barcelona, Brentford, Manchester City, Leeds United, Blackburn Rovers (L), Blackpool (L), Sheffield Wednesday (L)

International: Colombia

2023-24 Appearances: 2+8 for Leeds United & 8+2 on loan to Sheffield Wednesday

2023-24 Goals: 0

BLONDY NNA NOUKEU

Position: Goalkeeper

Date of Birth: 17 September 2001

Age at the Start of the Season: 22

Birthplace: Douala, Cameroon

Other Clubs: Royal Excel Mouscron, Stoke City, Crawley Town (L), Southend United (L)

International: Cameroon Under 21

2023-24 Appearances: 0

2023-24 Goals: 0

DID YOU KNOW?

Chris is on a season long loan from AFC Bournemouth who paid a reported £12m for him in 2019.

CHRIS MEPHAM

Position: Defender

Date of Birth: 5 November 1997

Age at the Start of the Season: 26

Birthplace: Harrow, London

Other Clubs: Chelsea, Brentford, AFC Bournemouth

International: Wales

2023-24 Appearances: 9+4 for AFC Bournemouth plus 6 for Wales

2023-24 Goals: 0

DID YOU KNOW?

Milan signed for Sunderland on his 19th birthday and scored twice in the Europa Conference League last season.

MILAN ALEKSIĆ

Position: Midfielder

Date of Birth: 30 August 2005

Age at the Start of the Season: 18

Birthplace: Kragujevac, Serbia

Other Clubs: FK Radnički 1923

International: Serbia

2023-24 Appearances: 16+9 for FK Radnički 1923

2023-24 Goals: 2 for FK Radnički1923

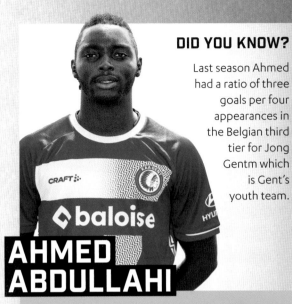

DID YOU KNOW?

Last season Ahmed had a ratio of three goals per four appearances in the Belgian third tier for Jong Gentm which is Gent's youth team.

AHMED ABDULLAHI

Position: Forward

Date of Birth: 19 June 2004

Age at the Start of the Season: 20

Birthplace: Nasarawa, Nigeria

Other Clubs: Gent

International: Nigeria Under 20

2023-24 Appearances: 0+1 for Gent & 28 for Jong Gent

2023-24 Goals: 21 for Jong Gent

DID YOU KNOW?

Currently on loan from Lens, Samed's first goal for his parent club was against Lorient who were managed by Régis le Bris.

SALIS ABDUL SAMED

Position: Midfielder

Date of Birth: 26 March 2000

Age at the Start of the Season: 24

Birthplace: Accra, Ghana

Other Clubs: JMG Academy, Clermont, Lens

International: Ghana

2023-24 Appearances: 24+11 for Lens & 8+3 for Ghana

2023-24 Goals: 0

PLAYER PROFILES

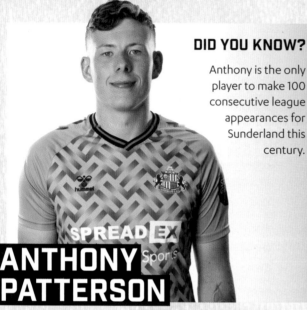

ANTHONY PATTERSON

DID YOU KNOW?

Anthony is the only player to make 100 consecutive league appearances for Sunderland this century.

Position: Goalkeeper

Date of Birth: 10 May 2000

Age at the Start of the Season: 24

Birthplace: Newcastle

Other Clubs: Sunderland RCA (L), Notts County (L)

International: None although has been called up to England U21 training camps

2023-24 Appearances: 46

2023-24 Goals: 0

Total SAFC Appearances: 123

Total SAFC Goals: 0

NATHAN BISHOP

DID YOU KNOW?

Nathan is spending the 2024-25 season on loan to Wycombe Wanderers.

Position: Goalkeeper

Date of Birth: 15 October 1999

Age at the Start of the Season: 24

Birthplace: Hillingdon, Greater London

Other Clubs: Southend United Manchester United, Mansfield Town (L), Wycombe Wanderers (L)

International: England Under 20

2023-24 Appearances: 2

2023-24 Goals: 0

Total SAFC Appearances: 2

Total SAFC Goals: 0

MATTY YOUNG

DID YOU KNOW?

Matty is spending the 2024-25 season on loan to Salford City.

Position: Goalkeeper

Date of Birth: 24 November 2006

Age at the Start of the Season: 17

Birthplace: Durham

Other Clubs: Darlington (L), Salford City (L)

International: England Under 18

2023-24 Appearances: 14 on loan to Darlington

2023-24 Goals: 0

Total SAFC Appearances: 0

Total SAFC Goals: 0

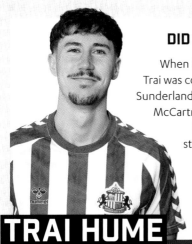

DID YOU KNOW?

When he was at Linfield, Trai was coached by former Sunderland full-back George McCartney and managed by ex-Sunderland striker David Healy.

TRAI HUME

Position: Full-back

Date of Birth: 18 March 2002

Age at the Start of the Season: 22

Birthplace: Ballymena

Other Clubs: Linfield, Ballymena United (L)

International: Northern Ireland

2023-24 Appearances: 46+1

2023-24 Goals: 1

Total SAFC Appearances: 78+6

Total SAFC Goals: 3

DID YOU KNOW?

Pembélé is on loan to Le Havre this season.

TIMOTHÉE PEMBÉLÉ

Position: Right-back

Date of Birth: 9 September 2002

Age at the Start of the Season: 21

Birthplace: Beaumont-sur-Oise, France

Other Clubs: US Persan 03, Paris Saint-Germain, Bordeaux (L), Le Havre (L)

International: France Under 20

2023-24 Appearances: 3+5

2023-24 Goals: 0

Total SAFC Appearances: 3+5

Total SAFC Goals: 0

DID YOU KNOW?

Mario Götze – the scorer of the winning goal in the 2014 FIFA World Cup final for Germany – and Liverpool striker Cody Gakpo were amongst Jenson's teammates when he made his debut for PSV.

JENSON SEELT

Position: Defender or holding midfielder

Date of Birth: 23 May 2023

Age at the Start of the Season: 21

Birthplace: Ede, Netherlands

Other Clubs: PSV Eindhoven

International: None

2023-24 Appearances: 11+6

2023-24 Goals: 0

Total SAFC Appearances: 11+6

Total SAFC Goals: 0

DID YOU KNOW?

Niall's goal against Watford was voted as Sunderland's goal of the season.

NIALL HUGGINS

Position: Full-back

Date of Birth: 18 December 2000

Age at the Start of the Season: 23

Birthplace: York

Other Clubs: Heworth, Leeds United

International: Wales Under 21

2023-24 Appearances: 18+2

2023-24 Goals: 1

Total SAFC Appearances: 22+6

Total SAFC Goals: 1

DENNIS CIRKIN

Position: Left-back

Date of Birth: 6 April 2002

Age at the Start of the Season: 22

Birthplace: Dublin

Other Clubs: Ridgeway Rovers, Tottenham Hotspur

International: England Under 20

2023-24 Appearances: 5+3

2023-24 Goals: 0

Total SAFC Appearances: 63+14

Total SAFC Goals: 5

DID YOU KNOW?

Dennis moved to England when he was three. He was born in Ireland and his parents are from Latvia.

LEO HJELDE

DID YOU KNOW?

Leo is the son of Jon Olav Hjelde who played for Nottingham Forest and once signed for South Korea's Busan IPark under manager Ian Porterfield – the goal-scorer in our 1973 FA Cup Final.

Position: Left-back / centre-back

Date of Birth: 26 August 2003

Age at the Start of the Season: 20

Birthplace: Nottingham

Other Clubs: Celtic, Ross County (L), Leeds United, Rotherham United (L)

International: Norway Under 21

2023-24 Appearances: 10+1

2023-24 Goals: 0

Total SAFC Appearances: 10+1

Total SAFC Goals: 0

AJI ALESE

DID YOU KNOW?

Aji played in the Europa League for West Ham United.

Position: Left-back / centre-back

Date of Birth: 17 January 2001

Age at the Start of the Season: 23

Birthplace: Islington, Greater London

Other Clubs: West Ham United, Accrington Stanley (L), Cambridge United (L)

International: England Under 20

2023-24 Appearances: 6+3

2023-24 Goals: 0

Total SAFC Appearances: 26+7

Total SAFC Goals: 1

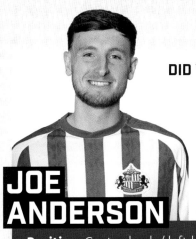

JOE ANDERSON

Position: Centre-back / left-back

Date of Birth: 6 February 2001

Age at the Start of the Season: 23

Birthplace: Stalybridge, Greater Manchester

Other Clubs: Liverpool, Everton, Shrewsbury Town (L)

International: None

2023-24 Appearances: 25+5, all on loan to Shrewsbury

2023-24 Goals: 0

Total SAFC Appearances: 0+4

Total SAFC Goals: 0

BEN CROMPTON

Position: Centre-back / right-back

Date of Birth: 17 December 2003

Age at the Start of the Season: 20

Birthplace: Telford

Other Clubs: Wolverhampton Wanderers, Shrewsbury Town

International: None

2023-24 Appearances: 0+1

2023-24 Goals: 0

Total SAFC Appearances: 0+1

Total SAFC goals: 0

DAN BALLARD

Position: Centre-back

Date of Birth: 22 September 1999

Age at the Start of the Season: 24

Birthplace: Stevenage

Other Clubs: Arsenal, Swindon Town (L), Blackpool (L), Millwall (L)

International: Northern Ireland

2023-24 Appearances: 44

2023-24 Goals: 3

Total SAFC Appearances: 65+1

Total SAFC Goals: 3

DID YOU KNOW?

When with Arsenal, Dan captained the Gunners to the final of the FA Youth Cup in 2018.

LUKE O'NIEN

Position: Centre-back

Date of Birth: 21 November 1994

Age at the Start of the Season: 29

Birthplace: Hemel Hempstead

Other Clubs: Watford, Wealdstone (L), Wycombe Wanderers

International: None

2023-24 Appearances: 44

2023-24 Goals: 2

Total SAFC Appearances: 233+32

Total SAFC Goals: 20

DID YOU KNOW?

O'Nien has played more games for Sunderland so far this century than any other player.

DID YOU KNOW?

Triantis is spending 2024-25 on loan to Hibernian.

NECTARIOS TRIANTIS

Position: Centre-back or holding midfielder

Date of Birth: 11 May 2003

Age at the Start of the Season: 21

Birthplace: Hurstville, Australia

Other Clubs: Canterbury Junior FC, Sydney Olympic, FNSW NTC, Sydney FC, West Sydney Wanderers, Central Coast Mariners, Hibernian (L)

International: Australia Under 23

2023-24 Appearances: 2+1 (plus 11+3 on loan to Hibernian)

2023-24 Goals: 0

Total SAFC Appearances: 2+1

Total SAFC Goals: 0

DID YOU KNOW?

Zak was only 16 years and 142 days old when he made his Sunderland debut.

ZAK JOHNSON

Position: Centre-back

Date of Birth: 25 May 2005

Age at the Start of the Season: 19

Birthplace: Sunderland

Other Clubs: Hartlepool United (L), Dundalk (L)

International: England Under 18

2023-24 Appearances: 1 (plus 11 on loan to Hartlepool United & 11+1 on loan to Dundalk)

2023-24 Goals: 0

Total SAFC Appearances: 1+1

Total SAFC Goals: 0

DAN NEIL

Position: Midfield	
Date of Birth: 13 December 2001	
Age at the Start of the Season: 22	
Birthplace: South Shields	
Other Clubs: None	
International: England Under 20	
2023-24 Appearances: 44	
2023-24 Goals: 4	
Total SAFC Appearances: 133+16	
Total SAFC Goals: 10	

DID YOU KNOW?

Dan is Sunderland's current Young Player of the Year.

DID YOU KNOW?

Pierre is on loan to Saint-Étienne during 2024-25.

PIERRE EKWAH

Position: Midfield

Date of Birth: 15 January 2002

Age at the Start of the Season: 22

Birthplace: Massy, France

Other Clubs: RC Arpajonnais, Brétigny FCS, CFF Paris, Nantes, Chelsea, West Ham United, Saint-Étienne (L)

International: France Under 20

2023-24 Appearances: 38+4

2023-24 Goals: 5

Total SAFC Appearances: 45+15

Total SAFC Goals: 5

DID YOU KNOW?

Jay is spending the 2024-25 season on loan to Bolton Wanderers.

JAY MATETE

Position: Midfield

Date of Birth: 11 February 2001

Age at the Start of the Season: 23

Birthplace: Lambeth, Greater London

Other Clubs: Reading, Fleetwood Town, Grimsby Town (L), Plymouth Argyle (L), Oxford United (L)

International: None

2023-24 Appearances: 0 (3+3 on loan to Oxford United)

2023-24 Goals: 0

Total SAFC Appearances: 14+11

Total SAFC Goals: 0

CHRIS RIGG

Position: Midfield

Date of Birth: 18 June 2007

Age at the Start of the Season: 17

Birthplace: Hebburn

Other Clubs: None

International: England Under 18

2023-24 Appearances: 9+13

2023-24 Goals: 3

Total SAFC Appearances: 9+16

Total SAFC Goals: 3

DID YOU KNOW?

Chris is Sunderland's youngest ever goal-scorer and youngest ever outfield player. He was 15 years and 203 days old when he first played at Shrewsbury in January 2023, and 16 years and 51 days old when he scored against Crewe Alexandra. That goal also made him the youngest scorer in the history of the League Cup.

DID YOU KNOW?

The skipper of the Under 21s, Harrison made his debut early this season in a Carabao Cup game at Preston North End.

HARRISON JONES

Position: Midfield

Date of Birth: 25 December 2004

Age at the Start of the Season: 19

Birthplace: York

Other Clubs: None

International: None

2023-24 Appearances: 0

2023-24 Goals: 0

Total SAFC Appearances: 0

Total SAFC Goals: 0

DID YOU KNOW?

Adil was the youngest player to ever start a Ligue 1 game for PSG when he debuted in a win at Metz in August 2019, when he was 17 years and 46 days old. He later became the youngest player to score in a cup-tie for the club.

ADIL AOUCHICHE

Position: Midfield

Date of Birth: 15 July 2002

Age at the Start of the Season: 22

Birthplace: Le Blanc-Mesnil, France

Other Clubs: Paris-Saint Germain, St. Etienne & Lorient

International: France Under 20

2023-24 Appearances: 10+18

2023-24 Goals: 2

Total SAFC Appearances: 10+18

Total SAFC Goals: 2

PATRICK ROBERTS

Position: Right-wing

Date of Birth: 5 February 1997

Age at the Start of the Season: 27

Birthplace: Kingston upon Thames

Other Clubs: AFC Wimbledon, Fulham, Manchester City, Celtic (L), Girona (L), Norwich City (L), Middlesbrough (L), Derby County (L), Troyes (L)

International: England Under 20

2023-24 Appearances: 21+11

2023-24 Goals: 0

Total SAFC Appearances: 65+32

Total SAFC Goals: 7

DID YOU KNOW?

Patrick scored against Manchester City in the Champions League in 2016 - while he was on loan from Manchester City to Celtic!

DID YOU KNOW?

The ex-Manchester City youngster made his debut in the Football League Trophy against Manchester United Under 21s and later came off the bench in a Carabao Cup game at Sheffield Wednesday in 2022.

CADEN KELLY

Position: Midfield

Date of Birth: 20 November 2003

Age at the Start of the Season: 20

Birthplace: Manchester

Other Clubs: Manchester City, Salford City

International: None

2023-24 Appearances: 0

2023-24 Goals: 0

Total SAFC Appearances: 0+2

Total SAFC Goals: 0

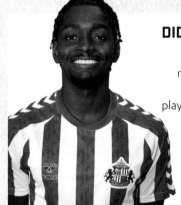

DID YOU KNOW?

Abdoullah has represented France at four age levels, playing 23 times for his country.

ABDOULLAH BA

Position: Winger / midfield

Date of Birth: 31 July 2003

Age at the Start of the Season: 21

Birthplace: Saint-Aubin-lés-Elbeuf, France

Other Clubs: CA Pîtres, Le Havre

International: France Under 20

2023-24 Appearances: 22+19

2023-24 Goals: 3

Total SAFC Appearances: 32+41

Total SAFC Goals: 4

JOBE

Position: Midfield or forward

Date of Birth: 23 September 2005

Age at the Start of the Season: 18

Birthplace: Stourbridge

Other Clubs: Birmingham City

International: England Under 20

2023-24 Appearances: 44+3

2023-24 Goals: 7

Total SAFC Appearances: 44+3

Total SAFC Goals: 7

DID YOU KNOW?

Jobe became the youngest player this century to score twice in a game for Sunderland when he netted a brace against Rotherham United last season.

DID YOU KNOW?

Although Romaine never got a first team game for Spurs, in 2021 he was on the bench alongside Jack Clarke for a Europa Conference League game in Portugal against Paços Ferreira.

ROMAIN MUNDLE

Position: Left-wing

Date of Birth: 24 April 2003

Age at the Start of the Season: 21

Birthplace: Edmonton, London

Other Clubs: Tottenham Hotspur, Standard Liège

International: None

2023-24 Appearances: 5+6 (plus 0+6 for Standard Liège)

2023-24 Goals: 1

Total SAFC Appearances: 5+6

Total SAFC Goals: 1

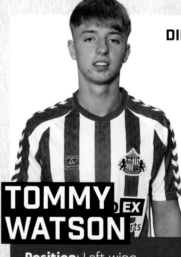

DID YOU KNOW?

Tommy has been with Sunderland since he was six.

TOMMY WATSON

Position: Left-wing

Date of Birth: 8 April 2006

Age at the Start of the Season: 18

Birthplace: Hartlepool

Other Clubs: None

International: England Under 18

2023-24 Appearances: 0+1

2023-24 Goals: 0

Total SAFC Appearances: 0+2

Total SAFC Goals: 0

JEWISON BENNETTE

Position: Left-wing

Date of Birth: 15 June 2004

Age at the Start of the Season: 20

Birthplace: Heredia, Costa Rica

Other Clubs: Herediano, Aris Thessaloniki (L)

International: Costa Rica

2023-24 Appearances: 1+1 (plus 2 for Aris and 1+1 for Costa Rica)

2023-24 Goals: 0

Total SAFC Appearances: 2+18

Total SAFC Goals: 2

LUÍS HEMIR SILVA SEMEDO

Position: Centre-forward

Date of Birth: 11 August 2003

Age at the Start of the Season: 20

Birthplace: Lisbon, Portugal

Other Clubs: Benfica, Juventus (L)

International: Portugal Under 20

2023-24 Appearances: 4+19

2023-24 Goals: 0

Total SAFC Appearances: 4+19

Total SAFC Goals: 0

NAZARIY RUSYN

Position: Forward

Date of Birth: 25 October 1998

Age at the Start of the Season: 25

Birthplace: Novoyavorivsk, Ukraine

Other Clubs: Lviv, Dynamo Kyiv, Zorya Luhansk (L), Legia Warsaw, Dnipro-1, Chornomorets Odesa (L), Zorya Luhansk

International: Ukraine Under 21

2023-24 Appearances: 10+12 (plus 2 for Zorya Luhansk)

2023-24 Goals: 2 +2 (plus 1 for Zorya Luhansk)

Total SAFC Appearances: 10+12

Total SAFC Goals: 2

ELIEZER MAYENDA

Position: Centre-forward

Date of Birth: 8 May 2005

Age at the Start of the Season: 19

Birthplace: Zaragoza, Spain

Other Clubs: Ebro, Breuillet FC., CS Brétigny, Sochaux, Hibernian (L)

International: Spain Under 17

2023-24 Appearances: 1+7 (plus 1+3 on loan to Hibernian)

2023-24 Goals: 0

Total SAFC Appearances: 1+7

Total SAFC Goals: 0

GAME TIME!

WHO AM I?

Can you name the players from the clues below? Use as few clues as possible.

1

....

....

2

....

....

3

....

....

Clues...

■ I was born in Le Blanc-Mesnil in France.

■ I joined Sunderland from Lorient in 2023.

■ I was the youngest player to start a game in Ligue 1 for Paris Saint-Germain when I played in a win at Metz in August 2019.

■ I scored nine goals in five games for France at the UEFA Under 17 Championship in 2019.

■ My surname contains all five vowels: A, E, I, O and U.

Clues...

■ I became the youngest player to score twice in a game for Sunderland this century when I played against Rotherham United in August 2023 when I was still 17.

■ My dad scored over 700 goals in non-league football.

■ I was still only 15 when I was first named on the bench for a first team game.

■ I was only 16 when I made my first team debut for Birmingham City.

■ My brother is a full England international.

Clues...

■ Mario Götze, the scorer of the winning goal in the 2014 FIFA World Cup Final, is a former teammate of mine.

■ So is Liverpool striker Cody Gakpo.

■ I can play at centre-back, full-back or in midfield.

■ I signed for Sunderland from PSV Eindhoven.

■ I was doing well for Sunderland in my first season until I got injured.

ODD ONE OUT

1

Which one of these players has **not** played in the Champions League..?

 Nazariy Rusyn

☐ Timothée Pembélé

☐ Patrick Roberts

2

Which one of these players has **not** played for Leeds United..?

☐ Niall Huggins

☐ Dennis Cirkin

☐ Jack Clarke

☐ Leo Hjelde

3

Which one of these players did **not** come through the Sunderland academy system..?

☐ Chris Rigg

☐ Romaine Mundle

☐ Dan Neil

☐ Anthony Patterson

SCRAMBLED

Can you unscramble these names to work out who the player is?

HERRP KAWIEE

1

STARK BEPORRTIC

2

NIK NEEOUL

3

NICKNAMES

Which Championship clubs have the following nicknames?

THE RAMS

1

THE BLADES

2

THE OWLS

3

FIND THE ANSWERS ON **PAGE 61**

SUNDERLAND SUPPORTER

TOM A. SMITH

Sunderland have had many celebrity supporters over the years – such as Dave Stewart, Sir Tim Rice and Steve Cram – and now they are about to have another one as local youngster Tom A. Smith makes his name in the music business.

"I think he's going to be a big star", said no less a figure than Sir Elton John after Tom supported him at Hyde Park in London while James, Johnny Marr and Richard Ashcroft are amongst the big names he has backed in 2024. Tom sang to the Sunderland squad at the club's End of Season Awards evening and has sang on the pitch at the Stadium of Light so listen out for the SAFC mad singer-songwriter.

■ **You're very passionate in performing your songs on stage Tom, would you say you are just as passionate in your support for the Lads?**

Yes absolutely, possibly even more so. I've been going to the football a lot longer than I've been appearing on stage. I started going to matches with my dad and grandad and I'm pretty sure I didn't miss a home game for about eight or nine years. We started in the Premier Concourse and then moved down to the South Stand.

I always wanted to be a footballer until I realised I was never going to be good enough!

■ **Who were your favourite players when you first started going to matches?**

Kenwyne Jones. My other favourites became Lee Cattermole, Seb Larsson, Connor Wickham and Asamoah Gyan. Later when I was on stage, sometimes I'd crack out an Asamoah Gyan dance! Even as a very young lad I used to write rap songs about Sunderland AFC, such as one about me being Connor Wickham's strike partner.

■ **You were once mascot in Martin O'Neill's first game – what can you remember about that?**

Connor Wickham realised I was just stood there before the match. He came and took me by the hand so I walked out with him. I'd have been seven years old. We won 2-1 and I was so excited.

■ **You have performed at some big gigs, such as Glastonbury, but how did singing for the squad at the end of season awards compare in terms of nervousness?**

It's up there. It's got to be number one really. Knowing you are playing in front of your heroes was really nerve-wracking. It went really well and I really enjoyed it.

Did you get to speak to any of the players and if so did you get any feedback on your performance?

I got to speak to quite a few players and they were genuinely nice. I had a good ten minutes chatting with Luke O'Nien. We were talking about how football and music were quite similar in that you had to work hard and put everything you've got into it. He told me he and his wife were going to put me on in the car on the way home so that was really cool. It was such a great night and it meant so much to be a part of it. The club have been so supportive of me over the last couple of years.

What was it like performing on the pitch at the Stadium of Light on Boxing Day 2022?

It was amazing. The whole day was fantastic and to walk out into the centre-circle to play one of my songs was really special. The feedback I got from that was incredible and interest sky-rocketed.

Your songs are often played on matchdays, how does that feel when you are in the ground?

The first time was the play-off semi-final against Sheffield Wednesday and that was so exciting. You go to the ground for so long and then to find

one of your songs being a contribution to matchday was incredible and so surreal.

Are any of the other members of the band local, and do they support SAFC?

We do have one Newcastle fan but I don't think they like football that much as they're really not that fussed, but the other two, Dylan and Fraser [the drummer and guitarist] are Sunderland fans as well. We all live about five minutes from each other. I went to East Rainton Primary School and then Houghton Kepier so I've grown up in the Houghton area.

Do you manage to follow the team when you are away on tour?

Absolutely yes. Everyone in the band will tell you that I irritate them by constantly giving them score updates from pretty much the entire league, and obviously I'm always there if I can be. Last season when Leeds were playing at Sunderland I was actually in Leeds but watched the match in a pub and kept quiet as we won 1-0.

How has your own year been in 2024?

I've had a busy time with festivals especially Kendal Calling, the Isle of White Festival and Summer Streets in Sunderland. I've also been supporting James as well as Johnny Marr, plus Richard Ashcroft from The Verve.

How about airplay on the radio?

I get quite a lot. Radio One have always been really supportive of what I've been doing over the last couple of years. I remember they played my first single just a few days after it was released.

Find Tom at:
www.tomasmithmusic.com
@tomasmithmusic

SAFC IN ESPAÑA

Sunderland warmed up for the 2024-25 season with a training camp in Spain. Two games were played at the Pinatar Arena in Murcia in south-eastern Spain.

These were part of warm weather training under the leadership of new head coach Regis Le Bris. SAFC started with a game against Premier League opposition in Nottingham Forest who they held to a 1-1 draw. Forest fought back to equalise after Sunderland went ahead with a penalty converted by Jack Clarke after Chris Rigg was brought down. The Lads also took on continental opposition in the shape of CD Eldense of Spain. In a match which witnessed first appearances for Alan Browne and Simon Moore, Sunderland won 2-1 with goals from academy product Tommy Watson and former Benfica youngster Hemir.

Watson's was a fine goal but Hemir's winner was a 25-yard scorcher hotter than the weather which meant the match had to be interrupted for drinks breaks.

SUNDERLAND WORE THEIR NEW AWAY KIT FOR THE FIRST TIME

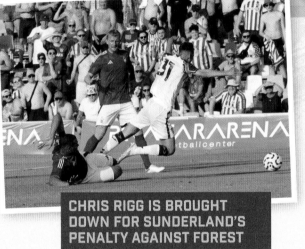

CLUB OWNER KYRIL LOUIS-DREYFUS

CHRIS RIGG IS BROUGHT DOWN FOR SUNDERLAND'S PENALTY AGAINST FOREST

HEMIR SCORES A SPECTACULAR WINNER AGAINST CD ELDENSE

Lots of supporters travelled to Spain to take in the games with many of them attending an open training session where they enjoyed the opportunity to meet the players and coaching staff. Sunderland also played five friendlies in England as part of their preparations for the season including one against Olympique de Marseille. This was a fixture played in honour of Robert Louis-Dreyfus, the father of Sunderland chairman Kyril Louis-Dreyfus. The father of Sunderland's owner was the majority shareholder of the French club from 1996 to 2009 during which time they reached a European final as well as two French finals. Because of improvements being made at the Stadium of Light the game with Olympique de Marseille was played at Bradford City, a ground which had also staged Sunderland against the host club a few days earlier.

SAFSHE

Sunderland's women's team were third in the Women's Championship in 2024. This was a huge improvement on the previous year as their points tally was more than twice as high as the previous season and brought an improvement of eight places in their league position. The Lasses did so well that until the last couple of fixtures, they were in with a serious chance of promotion.

Highlights of the campaign included an early season victory over highly fancied Southampton at St. Mary's where Jenna Dear despatched the only goal of the game. While that match was defensively tight, another highlight was a seven-goal thriller at home to Lewes where the girls refused to be beaten and stormed back to win despite trailing 2-3 with just three minutes to go. Once again it was Dear who was the matchwinner with two stunning late strikes.

GOLDEN GLOVE

Player of the Season Claudia Moan was named as the winner of the Barclays Women's Championship Golden Glove award having kept a remarkable 10 clean sheets in 22 league games, the last of these clean sheets coming away to champions Crystal Palace at Selhurst Park. "I'm really proud of myself and proud of the full squad, especially the back-line," Moan said. "It's what we wanted from the start of the season and we've came out and we've got it. I couldn't be prouder. It's not just about working with each other, we are all friends and we've all got that bond. That brings us together as a unit even more, we all want the same thing." Claudia left the club when her contract expired in the summer.

There were even more goals in the River Wear derby when near neighbours Durham were beaten 5-3 in front of a club record league crowd of 1,477. With players such as New Zealand's Katie Kitching and Mary McAteer of Wales being called up at international level the progress of the women's team has been very encouraging as they look to take the next step and mount another challenge to gain promotion to the Women's Super League.

UNDER 23 HAT-TRICK

Good news for the women's team is how well the Under 23s are doing as well, with more talent coming through. They won their league in style and also lifted the County Cup when goals from Mary Corbyn, Ella West and two from Jess Barker provided a 4-0 victory in the final against Norton & Stockton Ancients. Completing a fantastic hat-trick, goals from Niyah Dunbar and Niamh Boothroyd gave Courtney Lock's side a 2-1 victory over Barnsley in the final of the League Cup.

WOMEN'S RUGBY WORLD CUP

The summer of 2025 will see the Women's Rugby World Cup take place in England, with the Stadium of Light set to host matches in this prestigious global tournament.

Sunderland will stage the opening game of the competition on the evening of Friday 22 August when England will kick-off the World Cup on home soil.

Just over a month later the final will take place at the home of English rugby at Twickenham on Saturday 27 September. Other stadia being used in the tournament are Bristol City's Ashton Gate, Brighton & Hove Albion's Stadium, Sandy Park in Exeter, Franklin Gardens in Northampton, Salford Community Stadium in Manchester and York Community Stadium.

In addition to England, New Zealand, Canada and France were the first teams to qualify due to being the top four at the 2021 Women's Rugby World Cup. Sixteen teams will take part in what is the tenth time the trophy will have been competed for. New Zealand are the defending champions having defeated England in the last final.

■ Pictured: The USSR celebrate a goal against Italy at the football World Cup at Sunderland in 1966

1966

Way back in 1966 when England staged the association football World Cup Final, Sunderland's former ground of Roker Park staged three group matches and a quarter final. Italy, Chile, the USSR and Hungary all played at Sunderland.

"Women's Rugby World Cup England 2025 will be a generational moment for rugby," World Rugby's chairman, Sir Bill Beaumont, said. "The biggest, most accessible and most widely viewed, its unstoppable momentum will reach, engage and inspire new audiences in ways that rugby events have not done before. The selection of Sunderland for the opening match underscores that mission. We want this to be a sports event that everyone is talking about, that everyone wants to be a part of and one that inspires young people to be a part of."

The Leader of Sunderland City Council, Councillor Graeme Miller was just as enthusiastic about the announcement of the Stadium of Light as a World Cup venue. He said, "This is a fantastic announcement that will be welcomed by sports fans across the region. The city of Sunderland and the Stadium of Light will be once again seen on the world stage hosting a World Cup. Women's rugby – like women's sport in general – is growing in popularity, so to be able to support the England International Team at the Stadium of Light is an opportunity we know people locally will enjoy, and we're looking forward to welcoming fans from across the world to Sunderland."

The last Women's Rugby World Cup set new records for attendances. Over 150,000 fans attended games across the tournament with 1.8 million viewers on average tuned into the final while there were over 156 million video views on social media. The 2025 competition is set to smash these records with Sunderland being the starting point for a competition that will be followed worldwide and show the Stadium of Light to the globe.

RUGBY WORLD CUP 2021

RUGBY WORLD CUP 20

DELILAH DOES IT
HOW TO MAKE A FOOTBALL SCARF BIRTHDAY CAKE

INGREDIENTS

150g self-raising flour

500g white ready to roll icing sugar

150g caster sugar

250g red ready to roll icing sugar

150g soft margarine

200g jar of red jam

Three eggs

A few drops vanilla essence

YOU WILL ALSO NEED

A large mixing bowl

An electric mixer and an adult to help you with it, or a wooden spoon

A non-stick baking tin 210mm x 210mm

A rolling pin and a ruler

A small sharp knife which you have to be very careful with (get an adult to help you)

1. Wash your hands and turn on the oven to 180°/170° fan oven or 350°F electric, or gas mark 4.

2. Grease the baking tin with a little of the margarine.

3. Put all of the flour, margarine, sugar, eggs and vanilla essence into the mixing bowl. Very carefully switch on your mixer if you are using it and beat the ingredients together. Make sure you get rid of all the lumps until the mixture is pale and creamy. This will take a few minutes. If you are using a wooden spoon carefully mix the ingredients together then beat. This will take a few minutes longer than if you are using a mixer.

6 Measure your cake across the top and down both sides and roll the white icing to a rectangle this size.

7 Cover the cake the with jam and carefully lift the icing sugar over the cake and smooth it down. Trim the edges with your knife if needed.

4 Use a spoon to put the mixture into the baking tin, smoothing the surface when you have done this. Put the cake in the oven and bake for approximately 35-40 minutes until the cake is golden brown and cooked through. Carefully take the cake out of the oven using oven gloves and leave to cool completely for at least an hour and a half.

8 Roll out the red icing and cut into strips to make the stripes for the scarf. Keep two for the ends of the scarf and stick the rest evenly spaced across the cake. For the two remaining strips, cut a fringe along the long edge of each one as shown in the picture. Stick these on each end of the cake to finish your scarf. Your cake is now done.

You can add any decoration you wish like candles or write Happy Birthday with writing icing.

Enjoy your cake!

5 Take the cake out of the tin and cut in half lengthways to create two rectangles. Place them side by side and stick them together with a layer of jam to make one long rectangle. This will help the icing to stick to the cake.

THE BOSS

Sunderland had not had a head coach for many months but under three weeks after the end of the season, The Boss rolled into town. To music fans the world over The Boss means only one thing...

BRUCE SPRINGSTEEN

GLORY DAYS

The Stadium of Light has staged many world class shows over the years with some of music's biggest names. The Boss had played there before in 2012 while other megastars to have strutted their stuff at the SoL include: Beyonce, Take That, One Direction, Oasis, Coldplay and Rihanna. These and many others have put on great shows but maybe, just maybe this summer's Springsteen show was the best of them all.

It was summer in name only as the rain teemed down all night, soaking the crowd of over 40,000. It was far from the first time rain had tried to ruin a concert at the stadium but as with Bruce's previous appearance, and also when Coldplay excelled in horrendous conditions, the worst of the weather could not spoil the best of concerts. Even though the rain meant the start of the gig was delayed to help give the crowd time to get into the ground, Springsteen still played for over three hours, delivering 28 songs. He started with one he had

HUNGRY HEART

not played with his band for seven years, *Waiting on a Sunny Day*, trying to encourage the rain to stop.

Fronting a hugely talented band that included long term members Steve Van Zandt and Nils Lofgren, Springsteen included several songs suitable for a football team, such as *Born to Run* and *No Surrender*. Most importantly he played a song that hopefully will be appropriate at Sunderland in the not too distant future – *Glory Days*.

I'M ON FIRE

BORN TO RUN

WORLD CHAMPIONS

This painting by T.M.M. Hemy shows Sunderland in action in 1895, against Aston Villa.

In the very early days of football way back in the 1890s Sunderland were such a great team they became the World Champions! This happened 130 years ago this year, in 1895.

At this time football was just beginning in a few countries around the world. The sport was being introduced by British workers who had travelled abroad and started to help set up football teams. Only Scotland and England were really playing football to any great standard and so meetings between Scottish and English teams were big games.

For the first time in 1895 the League Champions of Scotland and England played each other in a match which was advertised as 'The Championship of the World'. The Cup Winners of the two countries had met before. The Football League had started in 1888-89 with the Scottish League playing its first season in 1890-91.

Hearts were the Scottish Champions and Sunderland were Champions of England. Known as 'The Team of All The Talents' Sunderland had just won the league for the third time in four seasons. They had been runners-up in 1894 having won the title in 1892 and 1893, before regaining it in 1895.

The match for the World Championship was played at Hearts' ground in Edinburgh on 27 April 1895. Sunderland won the match 5-3. Not just the home team were full of Scottish players. Sunderland's line-up was also made up entirely of Scotsmen. One of Sunderland's top players was forward Johnny Campbell. In becoming a World Champion with Sunderland, he became the only player to become a World Champion with both an English team and a Scottish one. Seven years earlier he had played in a match between the Scottish and English cup winners, being part of a side called Renton who defeated West Bromwich Albion when those clubs were both cup holders.

Johnny Campbell was 'The Team of All The Talents' greatest goal machine.

John Auld was the first captain of The Team of All The Talents.

John Harvie was also on the mark in the match that made Sunderland World Champions.

In the Hearts v Sunderland World Championship game, Sunderland led 2-0 at half time but then had to come from behind after Hearts showed their ability by taking a 3-2 lead. It was not unusual in those days to have some dispute as to who scored the goals, but the Sunderland goals are believed to have been scored by Johnny Campbell, who got two (although some reports claim one of these was scored by Jamie Millar), Harry Johnston, Jamie Millar and John Harvie.

Earlier in this season, the artist Thomas Marie Madawaska Hemy painted what is thought to be the world's oldest and biggest oil painting of an association football match. The painting shows a match at Sunderland's ground of the time with Aston Villa. The enormous painting is now in the entrance hall of the Stadium of Light so every player who ever comes to the stadium, even now in 2025, has a reminder of 'The Team of All The Talents' who made Sunderland World Champions.

Photograph by THE SUNDERLAND PHOTOGRAPHIC CO.,
SUNDERLAND ASSOCIATION FOOTBALL CLUB COMMITTEE AND PLAYERS.
WINNERS OF LEAGUE CHAMPIONSHIP.—SEASON 1894-95.

W. WALLACE, (Fin. Sec.)   T. DODDS, (Trainer)   R. McNEIL.   J. E. DOIG.   H. WILSON.   D. GOW.   A. McCREADIE.   Mr. JAS. HENDERSON.   H. REYNOLDS, (Groundsman)
Mr. T. POTTS.   T. WATSON, (Sec.)   W. DUNLOP.   J. MILLER.   J. HANNAH.   J. HARVIE,   Coun. J. P. HENDERSON, (Presid.)   Coun. T. MARSHALL,
J. AULD.   J. GILLESPIE.   J. CAMPBELL.   J. SCOTT.   H. JOHNSTON.   Mr. S. WILSON.

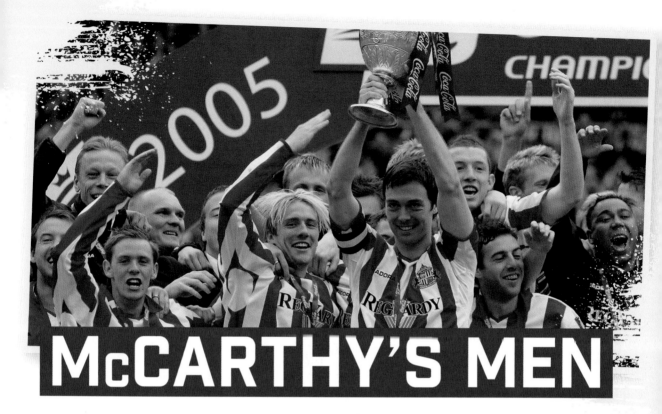

McCARTHY'S MEN

2004-05 CHAMPIONSHIP CHAMPIONS

Twenty years ago this season, Sunderland won the Championship in 2004-05. What's more, the team achieved this with 94 points – the second highest number of points SAFC have ever gained in a season. 105 in 1998-99 is the record.

Managed by Mick McCarthy, Sunderland had narrowly missed out on promotion a year earlier. The Lads had lost on penalties in the play-off semi-finals and had been beaten 1-0 by Millwall in the FA Cup semi-final. 2004-05 was to be a season of success as Sunderland steadily climbed the table after a slow start.

1 Longest run of consecutive league defeats

Just one win and three defeats with two draws in the opening six league game meant a sluggish start before the first international break. Manager McCarthy was mightily frustrated at this point but his team clicked into gear after the break and scored three times in the first 20 minutes as they went on to win 4-0 at Gillingham, with a hat-trick from Marcus Stewart. Victory was the first of four in a row in the league. From then on, the longest the team went without a win was two league games as

94 Points – the second highest in Sunderland's history

the side found the consistency needed to top the table.

A sequence of six wins in seven games during the autumn put a rocket under the red and whites as they zoomed up the league. This was bettered in the spring when eight wins in a row climaxed at nearest rivals Wigan

76 Goals	**29** Wins	**13** Debutants	**30** Players used	**4** Goalies used

who would be runners up. Sunderland's vast support on a Tuesday night almost doubled the Latics average home gate in giving Wigan their biggest attendance of the season, as almost 21,000 saw Marcus Stewart score the only goal of a key match.

16 League goals for top scorer **Marcus Stewart**

An injury to Norway international goalkeeper Thomas Myhre meant he had to go off in the next game which was surprisingly lost at home to Reading. Myhre was replaced by Northern Irishman Michael Ingham but when he had a tough time next time out in a draw at promotion rivals Ipswich Town, McCarthy took the bold decision to leave him out in favour of 18-year old debutant Ben Alnwick for a crucial home encounter with Leicester City. Within five minutes Alnwick was beaten by Alan Maybury and people worried Sunderland were going to miss out on promotion once again. Alnwick though proved a hero with a couple of excellent saves before Sunderland gained their

37 YEARS **58** DAYS

SAFC's oldest ever debutant – Brian Deane

composure, equalised through Marcus Stewart and scored a second half winner when Steve Caldwell rose highest to power home a header from a Liam Lawrence corner.

As the final whistle sounded Sunderland hoped they were promoted but did not know for certain. They needed third placed Ipswich to drop points at Leeds. There was an agonising wait for the result to come through from Elland Road. When it did the score was Leeds United 1-1 Ipswich Town, leaving the Tractor Boys seven points behind with only six to play for. Sunderland were up but there was still the title up for grabs.

The following Friday night, in front of a live TV audience and West Ham United's biggest gate of the season, Sunderland trailed the sixth placed Hammers at half time. They went on to win and seal the Coca-Cola Championship with Stephen 'Sleeves' Elliott scoring a superb late winner after Julio Arca had equalised.

A capacity crowd of over 47,000 turned up at the final match

9 Points clear of third place

of the campaign. They saw the trophy raised by Gary Breen after a goal from Wales international Carl Robinson was enough to beat Stoke City and take the season's points tally to that impressive 94.

Captain Gary Breen, his centre-back partner Steve Caldwell, midfielder Carl Robinson and striker Marcus Stewart all played at least 40 league matches with another six players topping 30 league appearances as McCarthy's men won the title in style.

END OF MONTH POSITIONS

August	17th
September	7th
October	5th
November	3rd
December	2nd
January	3rd
February	2nd
March	1st
April	1st
May	1st

SAFC FRANCE

Pictured left to right: Adil Aouchiche, Pierre Ekwah, Timothée Pembélé & Abdoullah Ba

France are modern day football giants. They have been in four of the last seven FIFA World Cup Finals, winning the trophy in 2018 and 1998 and only losing the finals of 2006 and 2022 on penalties.

Since Sunderland moved to the Stadium of Light in 1997 there have been enough French players in red and white to make up more than two teams. In addition to those there have been more than enough players who have played in French football and for Sunderland that you could make up a third team. You could also have a manager and a coach. Mick McCarthy, who led Sunderland to the Championship title in 2005 had played for Lyon while Eric Black who was caretaker boss at Sunderland had played for Metz. In the summer of 2024, Brittany-born Régis Le Bris became Sunderland's head coach with one of his signings being France U20 international forward Wilson Isidor.

Of Sunderland's modern day French footballers, Timothée Pembélé played for France at the 2020 Olympics and lined up alongside Lionel Messi, Kylian Mbappe and Neymar when he was at Paris Saint-Germain. Adil Aouchiche became the youngest player to start a Ligue 1 game for PSG. He has also been capped by France at junior levels, as have Abdoullah Ba and Pierre Ekwah.

SUNDERLAND'S STRONGEST FRENCH XI

PEREZ

CARTERON

KABOUL

KONE

REVIEILLERE

MALBRANQUE

BASSILA

M'VILA

ROY

CISSE

SAHA

LIONEL PEREZ
A teammate of Eric Cantona and Zinedine Zidane in French club football, Lionel made one of the greatest double-saves made by a Sunderland goalie in the semi-final of a 1998 play-off game with Sheffield United.

PATRICE CARTERON
Scored a great goal against Newcastle in 2001 when on loan from St. Etienne. He went on to be a highly successful manager, especially in Africa.

YOUNES KABOUL
Capped five times by France, Kaboul formed a brilliant partnership with Lamine Kone as Sunderland stayed in the Premier League in 2016.

LAMINE KONE
Paris born defender who played for France at Under 21 level before winning full caps with Ivory Coast, the country of his parents.

ANTONY REVEILLERE
Full back with 20 caps for France. He came to Sunderland as a veteran in 2014 after being part of the Lyon line-up who won Ligue 1 for five successive seasons.

STEED MALBRANQUE
Born in Belgium but a fantastically skilful Under 21 international for France. He was twice in squads for the full national side without being capped.

CHRISTIAN BASSILA
Powerful Paris-born midfielder who played at Under 21 level for France and captained Guingamp to triumph in the French Cup in 2009, three years after leaving Sunderland.

YANN M'VILA
22 caps for France and a superb season with SAFC in 2015-16.

ERIC ROY
The son of a former France international, Eric was a quality midfielder who went on to be a manager in his home country.

DJIBRIL CISSE
Scored nine goals in 41 games for France and played at the 2010 FIFA World Cup finals. Scored in both matches against Newcastle in 2008-09 during a season on loan from Olympique de Marseille.

LOUIS SAHA
Striker who played for France in the semi-final of the 2006 FIFA World Cup final but was suspended for the final.

HOME COMFORTS

During the close season SAFC invested in upgrading the Stadium of Light with a multi-million pound improvement programme.

The stadium was opened in 1997 and is now benefiting from maintenance and modernisation. After Quinn's Bar, The Montgomery Suite, the Business Lounge and executive boxes were extensively upgraded last year, this summer the highest level of stadium investment in over two decades was aimed at improving the matchday experience for supporters.

- A new public address (P.A) system. Previously, in some parts of the ground it was very difficult to hear what was being announced in the stadium but now there is a brand new state of the art sound system.

- New floodlights befitting a ground called the Stadium of Light. The new lights are able to create light shows and be connected to the music played on the new sound system. The LED floodlights introduced by Sunderland have been used at clubs in Germany and Argentina, including the world-famous Boca Juniors.

SAFC Chief Business Officer David Bruce shows chairman Kyril Louis-Dreyfus this season's home kit.

↑ SAFC Chief Business Officer David Bruce announces the opening of the spectacular new club store.

- A brand new pitch and undersoil heating system were installed to try and give the team a first class playing surface.

- The club shop at the stadium has been moved to a much bigger, brighter and exciting store in the Black Cat House administration building next to the stadium. Operated by Fanatics who have agreed a 10 year partnership with the club the club's store and online store are set to become a massive improvement for Sunderland fans.

- New ticketing points have been created on the north east corner of the stadium.

- In partnership with Sunderland City Council, work is also continuing to develop the city's 5G network, which will see the Stadium of Light become the first 5G enabled football stadium in the United Kingdom in 2025.

STAND UP IF YOU LOVE 'SUN-LUN'

One of the biggest changes to the stadium is that from the 2024-25 season, for the first time since the Stadium of Light opened, fans will be able to have a standing place rather than a seat. Safe standing has been introduced with 2,000 standing places in the Roker End and a further 1,000 in the North Stand upper.

QUIZ
OF THE YEAR

1 Which team was beaten 2-0 at the Stadium of Light on New Year's Day in 2024?

2 What did Chelsea and Barnsley have in common last season?

3 Which former Tottenham youngster did Sunderland sign from a Belgian club at the start of the year?

4 Name the Norway Under-21 international defender signed from Leeds United in January.

5 Who was the Sunderland Player of the Century who sadly passed away in April?

6 Ten players appeared in the Premier League during the 2023-24 season who have played for Sunderland or been academy players at the club.

Give yourself a point for each one you can name. If you get all ten correct award yourself double marks!

7 Which of the clubs promoted to the Premier League in 2024 were beaten 5-0 by Sunderland last season?

8 Which of these clubs did not finish on the same number of points as Sunderland last season: Swansea City, Watford, Stoke City or QPR?

9 Who was Sunderland's Young Player of the year in 2023-24?

10 Which Scottish Premiership team took two players on loan from Sunderland in the second half of last season?

11 Who were the two players? One was from Australia and the other from Spain.

12 Who was Sunderland's head coach at the start of 2024?

13 Who took over from him as interim head coach?

14 Name the winger who played at the 2022 FIFA World Cup who went on loan to a Greek club.

15 Name the Northern Ireland international club captain released at the end of the 2023-24 season.

16 Who did Sunderland Under-21s play in the PL2 final?

17 Which American superstar staged a concert at the Stadium of Light in May?

18 Which country did Sunderland travel to in pre-season?

19 Who was the first Championship fixture of 2024-25 against?

20 Who scored Sunderland's first goal of the 2024-25 season?

FIND THE ANSWERS ON PAGE 61

YOUR SCORE

FOUNDATION OF LIGHT

Foundation of Light is the charity belonging to Sunderland AFC.

Specialising in more than just football, the Foundation is made up of teachers, health workers, coaches, family learning officers, youth workers and support staff that work with over 20,000 people across Sunderland and beyond every year.

The Foundation works with people as young as babies of 18 months to adults of over 80 and offers activities for everyone; with courses to help health and wellbeing, behaviour, attitude, skills, knowledge and much more.

Whilst being linked to SAFC, the Foundation is independent from the football club and responsible for fundraising £4 million each year to run their life-changing programmes.

The players are always more than happy to lend their support to the work that the Foundation does and can be regularly seen in the Beacon of Light, the Foundation's home.

Corry Evans, Bradley Dack and Nectar Triantis and SAFC Women's stars Mary McAteer and Liz Ejupi joined youngsters enjoying their school holidays at the Beacon.

Pierre Ekwah is a regular in the kitchen, dropping in to cook with families. Aji Alese was also spotted in the kitchen at Halloween helping whip up some spooky treats!

Dennis Cirkin and Elliot Embleton got the chance to meet supporters in the SAFC Fan Zone, with Dennis also joining a disability football session.

Trai Hume and Niall Huggins helped to hand out awards at the Foundation's annual Gala Dinner and Dan Ballard dressed up as Where's Wally on World Book Day.

ABOUT THE FOUNDATION OF LIGHT

500,000
Worked with over 500,000 people since being formed in 2001 by Sir Bob Murray

40
Has 40 different courses to support local young people and their families

240
Supports over 240 local schools with PE, literacy and numeracy

6,000
Over 6,000 visitors to the Beacon of Light every week

For more information visit **foundationoflight.co.uk** or scan the QR code:

TOP 10
MOST EXPENSIVE
PLAYERS

Many people think that Didier N'Dong's £13.6m move to Sunderland in 2016 makes him the club's record signing but, with add-ons, Darren Bent's move from Spurs in 2009 makes him the most expensive player Sunderland have bought at a total of £16.5m.

WHO ARE THE MOST EXPENSIVE PLAYERS TO HAVE PLAYED FOR SUNDERLAND?

All fees quoted here are the maximums from reported transfer deals. The fees are the ones that were reported at the times of the transfers if all add-ons were fulfilled. Sometimes these fees are never paid in full as add-ons tend to depend on things such as how many appearances are made and how well the team does after a player moves.

£37M

AMAD DIALLO ATALANTA
TO MANCHESTER UNITED 2021

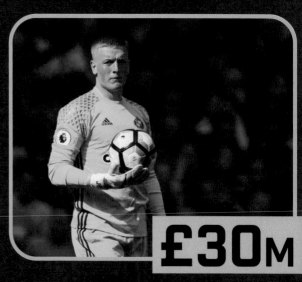

£30M

JORDAN PICKFORD
TO EVERTON 2017

£24M

MARCOS ALONSO FIORENTINA
TO CHELSEA 2016

£24M

**DARREN BENT TO ASTON VILLA 2011
& £16.5M TOTTENHAM HOTSPUR TO
SUNDERLAND 2009**

£20M

JACK CLARKE
SUNDERLAND TO
IPSWICH TOWN 2024

£16M

JORDAN HENDERSON
TO LIVERPOOL 2011

£16M

DANNY WELBECK
MANCHESTER UNITED
TO ARSENAL 2014

£15M

JACK RODWELL
EVERTON TO
MANCHESTER CITY 2012

£14M

DJIBRIL CISSE
AUXERRE TO
LIVERPOOL 2004

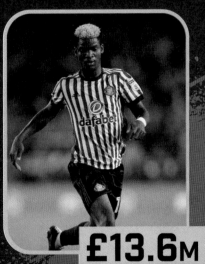

£13.6M

**DIDIER NDONG LORIENT
TO SUNDERLAND 2016**

GAME TIME 2

EYE DENTITY

Can you identify these players from looking into their eyes?

1

2

3

4

SPOT THE SCORE

Can you match the games to the score-line? All the games are from 2024. The scores were: **0-1, 0-2, 2-0, 3-1 and 3-1** but which one goes with which game?

1. Sunderland ☐☐ Preston North End
2. Sunderland ☐☐ Stoke City
3. Sunderland ☐☐ Plymouth Argyle
4. Cardiff City ☐☐ Sunderland
5. West Bromwich Albion ☐☐ Sunderland

SPOT THE DIFFERENCE

Can you spot eight differences from when Sunderland took on Sheffield Wednesday?

TAKE TWO

Can you work out which two players have contributed to each face?!

1

2

LUKE
O'NIEN

WHO AM I? P30

1 - Adil Aouchiche
2 - Jobe Bellingham
3 - Jenson Seelt

ODD ONE OUT P30

1 - Nazariy Rusyn, who has played in the Europa League but not the Champions League.
2 - Dennis Cirkin
3 - Romaine Mundle

SCRAMBLED P30

1 - Pierre Ekwah
2 - Patrick Roberts
3 - Luke O'Nien

NICKNAMES P30

1 - Derby County
2 - Sheffield United
3 - Sheffield Wednesday

EYE-DENTITY P58

1 - Aji Alese
2 - Luke O'Nien
3 - Adil Aouchiche
4 - Jenson Seelt

SPOT THE SCORE P58

1 - Sunderland **2-0** Preston North End
2 - Sunderland **3-1** Stoke City
3 - Sunderland **3-1** Plymouth Argyle
4 - Cardiff City **0-2** Sunderland
5 - West Bromwich Albion **0-1** Sunderland

TAKE TWO P59

Face 1
Jobe Bellingham
Luis Hemir

Face 2
Nazariy Rusyn
Patrick Roberts

ANSWERS

QUIZ OF THE YEAR P52-53

1 - Preston North End
2 - They both loaned a player to Sunderland. Chelsea loaned Mason Burstow while Barnsley loaned Callum Styles.
3 - Romaine Mundle
4 - Leo Hjelde
5 - Charlie Hurley
6 - Remi Matthews (Crystal Palace)
Antoine Semenyo (AFC Bournemouth)
Jason Steele & Danny Welbeck (Brighton & Hove Albion)
Mason Burstow (Chelsea)
Jordan Pickford (Everton)
James McConnell (Liverpool, former SAFC Academy player)
Amad Diallo & Jonny Evans (Man Utd)
John Egan (Sheffield United)

7 - Southampton
8 - Swansea City
9 - Dan Neil
10 - Hibernian
11 - Nectarios Triantis and Eliezer Mayenda
12 - Michael Beale
13 - Mike Dodds
14 - Jewison Bennette
15 - Corry Evans
16 - Tottenham Hotspur
17 - Bruce Springsteen
18 - Spain
19 - Cardiff City
20 - Luke O'Nien

SPOT THE DIFFERENCE P59

ELIEZER
MAYENDA